THIS WALKER BOOK BELONGS TO:

To Stephanie

Love Stew xxx

~~Lorastew~~

Buckingham

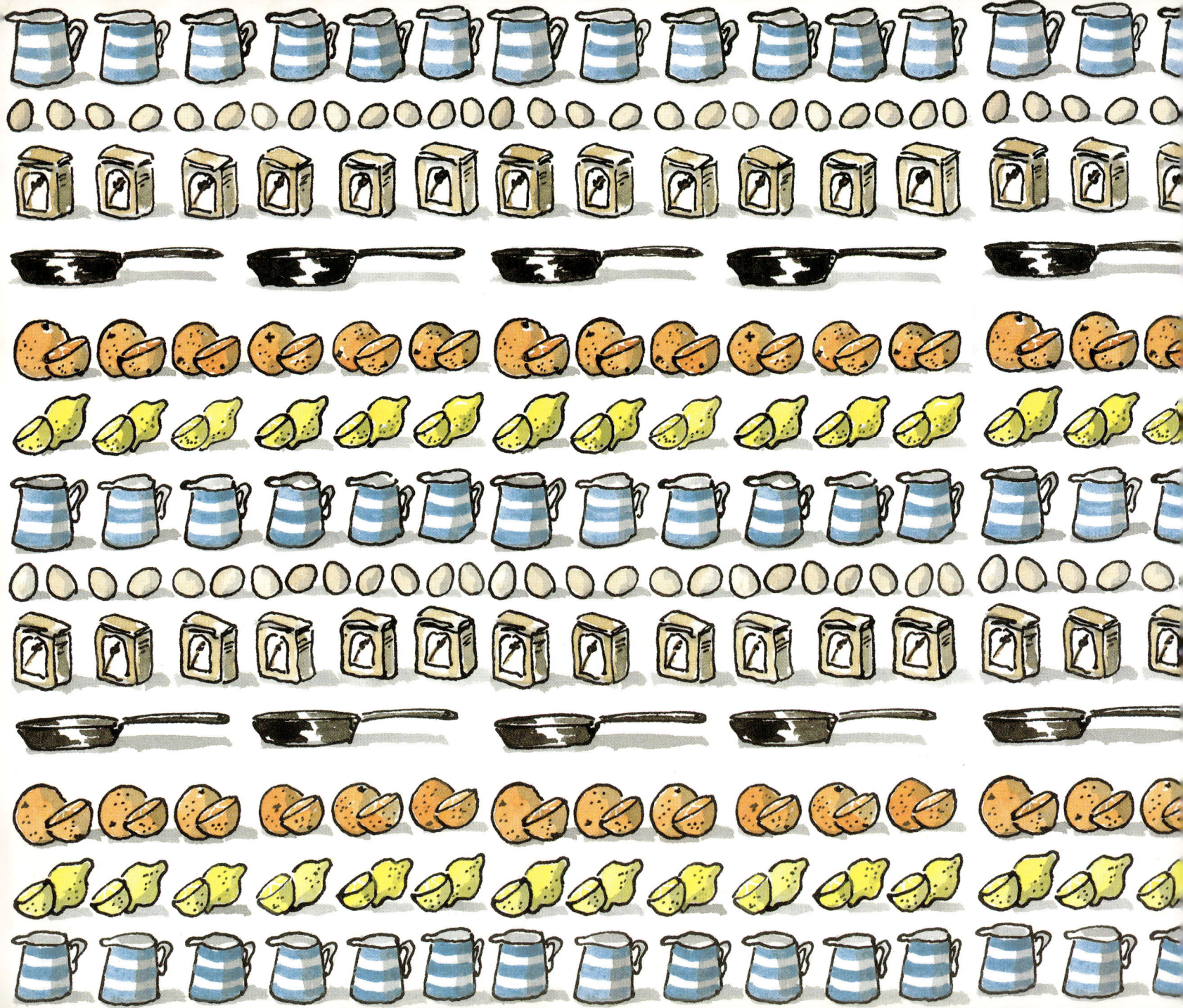

For Harry and Lucy
(two very young farmers)

First published 1990 by Julia MacRae Books
This edition published 1991 by Walker Books Ltd
87 Vauxhall Walk, London SE11 5HJ

© 1990 Caroline Crossland

Printed in Hong Kong by
Sheck Wah Tong Printing Press Ltd

British Library Cataloguing in Publication Data
Patrick's perfect pancake.
I. Title
823'.914[J]
ISBN 0-7445-1603-X

PATRICK'S PERFECT PANCAKE

Caroline Crossland

WALKER BOOKS
LONDON

Patrick was a chef. He worked long hours in the kitchen of a great hotel and as he worked he dreamed about green fields and cows. Patrick didn't really want to be a chef. He wanted to be a farmer. And so one day he packed his bags and went off into the country. He bought a small farm, a handful of chickens, and seven cows, each one of them different from the other.

He gave them all names, down to the very last chicken, and spent many happy hours talking to them about his days in the hotel kitchen. Patrick's animals were contented and peaceful. They knew how lucky they were to have Patrick looking after them.

The cows on the neighbouring farms were not content at all. Nobody talked to them or wondered if they were happy. Their masters laughed at Patrick. "Fancy letting your chickens run all over the place!" they said to him. "Why don't you keep them cooped up in

cages as we do? You could have ten times as many. Profit and
Productivity, that's what it's all about."
Patrick didn't know what Profit and Productivity were, but he did
know that *his* chickens were happy.

One day Patrick was reading his CHEF'S WEEKLY (which he still ordered from habit) when he saw a very interesting announcement:

CLASSIFIED

Wanted

One Jelly Mould in shape of Rabbit.
Contact Tom 3164791

...ackbird
...r Apple Pies etc.
...rnest 20913

...ocolate Cake Recipe
...Mine mislaid.)
Box no. 3092

For Sale

Pink Oven Gloves (unwanted gift: unused.)
Contact Dexter: 372 7732

Onions on strings (Also some garlic)
Contact Pierre: 2094 23770

Knife Sharpener (Mind your fingers)
Alfie: 526 7294

ANNOUNCEMENT

PANCAKE COMPETITION
OPEN TO ALL CHEFS
APPLY TO THE PALACE
(Prize: Golden Frying Pan)

We are pleased to ann... the result of our wooden s... raffle. The lucky win... Peter Ladle, ticket no. 82...

Patrick sat down at once and wrote out his application.

Then he began to practise making pancakes, using the milk and eggs provided by his own dear cows and chickens. He tried different recipes and he tried all his pans, one after the other, until he found the one which suited him best.

"I've done it!" he cried later, and he rushed outside to tell the animals that he had made the best pancake ever.

After three days a letter came from the Palace.
Patrick had been chosen for the competition! He ran round
and round the farmyard patting each of the seven cows and all
of the chickens in turn.
"I'm going to London tomorrow to cook for the Queen," he said,
"and you must give me the finest milk and eggs in all the land."

For the rest of that day Patrick busily prepared everything he would need. In a big suitcase he packed his ...

chef's hat and apron,
his pyjamas and toothbrush,

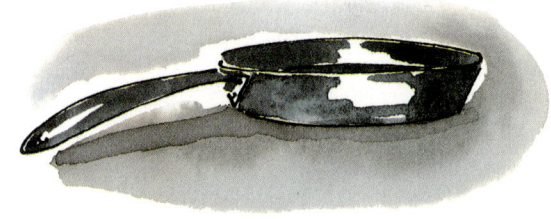

his favourite frying pan,

and a photograph of the farm
just in case he got homesick.
He gathered all the eggs he could find from every nook and cranny, and he herded the cows into the barn for a final milking. Then he said goodnight to all the animals, made sure they had enough food for the time he was away, and thanked them for all their hard work.

Early next morning Patrick climbed into his old van with his suitcase, a box of eggs, and a churn of milk.

When he arrived in London a policeman directed him to the Palace. There he was shown to the Royal kitchens by a butler, and he met the three other chefs in the competition.

One was a big Scot; the second was a small Frenchman; and the third was an elderly man with thick glasses. They all had their eggs and milk in front of them. The milk was in cartons and the eggs were gleaming and clean, unlike Patrick's eggs which had bits of mud and feather stuck to them. But Patrick didn't mind, because it calmed his nerves to think of his friendly hens back home.

All the chefs were given numbers.
Patrick was Number Two.
A whistle blew and they
each began to work.
There was no sound except
the cracking of eggs and
the beating of whisks.
Patrick knew the first few
pancakes would stick
(they always do)
but before long all the
chefs began turning out
thin golden discs,
lacy and pale brown
around the edges.

At six o'clock the butler came back.
"It's time to stop," he said.
The pancakes were piled on to four plates,
and a flag with a number on top was stuck
into each pile.
Then four footmen appeared and
each carried a plate away to the Queen's
Banqueting Hall at the other end of the Palace.

The four chefs sat in the kitchen trying not to bite their nails with anxiety. Which one of them would win? The butler came in. "Will Chef Number Two please come with me," he said. Patrick's knees knocked as he followed the butler down the long corridor to the Banqueting Hall. When he got there he swept off his hat and bowed low.

"Patrick," said the Queen from her red velvet throne,
"I must tell you that yours are the best pancakes I have ever tasted.
There's a fresh-air flavour about them, they are altogether
happier-tasting than the others. Quite delightful.
You have won the competition with your perfect pancakes."
The Queen shook Patrick by the hand and left the room as he bowed
again. He couldn't believe his luck!
He had won, thanks to the unique ingredients of his pancakes.

When he left the Palace he found reporters and television cameras at the gate. Everyone wanted to know about his pancakes.
He had to stay in London for a few more days answering questions and having his picture taken. In all the excitement he quite forgot the farm and the animals back home.

The cows and the chickens waited in vain for Patrick to return. They were lonely and fed-up, and besides they wanted to know how Patrick had got on. The cows mooed and the chickens clucked.

"What's the matter?" said a fat London pigeon who had flown into the country for a rest. And when he heard the story of the missing Patrick he said at once, "Why, that must be the famous chef who won the Pancake Competition in London."

The cows and chickens mooed and clucked more loudly than ever, furious that Patrick had not come home to tell them the news.

The pigeon, who seemed to know everything, told them that there was to be a big television interview with Patrick that evening. "Come on," he said, "we've just got time to get there if you follow me."

And so a procession set off for London, making its way through the countryside, past houses and schools and churches and parks and into the centre of London, arriving at Piccadilly Circus in the

rush-hour. Nobody could stop them. Policemen waved their arms,
but the cows and the chickens went on following the pigeon.
They were all slightly tired by now, but they kept going until they
reached the television studio.

At seven o'clock, just as Patrick came on to the stage in front of a cheering audience, the animals burst through the studio doors. The whole country saw a most touching reunion take place as Patrick, hardly believing his eyes, hugged as many cows and chickens as he could manage.

They were a forgiving lot, and were so pleased to see Patrick again that they didn't get cross with him for abandoning them. Patrick, whose head had been a bit turned by his sudden fame, was so impressed by their long journey to find him that all he wanted to do was go back to the farm with them as soon as possible.

He looked at the camera.
"I owe everything to these friends," he said.

"If they hadn't produced the milk and the eggs I couldn't have made the pancakes. It's all due to them, and they deserve a happy life."
With that he followed the animals out of the studio, as they were getting a bit hot, and they all went home.

Patrick's neighbours, who had been watching him on television, were ashamed that they had laughed at him. They let out all their chickens, who have roamed free from that day to this.
And sometimes (when they are sure no one is looking) they even have a few quick chats with their cows.

MORE WALKER PAPERBACKS
For You to Enjoy

GIANT
by Juliet and Charles Snape

Shortlisted for the Smarties Book Prize
A compelling ecological fairy tale for today on the theme of caring for our environment.
"A powerful picture book." *The Sunday Times*
ISBN 0-7445-1441-X   £2.99

FARMER BUNGLE FORGETS
by Dick King-Smith/Martin Honeysett

No matter what Mrs Bungle asks him to do, Farmer Bungle just can't remember – with disastrous results.
"Nice sense of involvement as the reader wills the farmer to remember." *The Sunday Telegraph*
ISBN 0-7445-1777-X   £2.99

"QUACK!" SAID THE BILLY-GOAT
by Charles Causley/Barbara Firth

When the cow is going "baa" and the hen is going "oink", the farmer himself must be quackers!
"Every word in the right place, and a lovely joke at the end." *Martin Waddell, The Irish News*
0-7445-1442-8   £2.99

Walker Paperbacks are available from most booksellers, or by post from Walker Books Ltd, PO Box 11, Falmouth, Cornwall TR10 9EN.

To order, send:
Title, author, ISBN number and price for each book ordered, your full name and address and a cheque or postal order for the total amount, plus postage and packing:

UK, BFPO and Eire – 50p for first book, plus 10p for each additional book to a maximum charge of £2.00.
Overseas Customers – £1.25 for first book, plus 25p per copy for each additional book.
Prices are correct at time of going to press, but are subject to change without notice.